POP ART
★ IN MY GALLERY ★

WRITTEN BY
EMILIE DUFRESNE

DESIGNED BY
DANIELLE RIPPENGILL

Published in 2022 by Enslow Publishing, LLC
101 W. 23rd Street, Suite 240,
New York, NY 10011

Copyright © 2020 Booklife Publishing
This edition published by arrangement with Booklife Publishing

All rights reserved.

No part of this book may be reproduced by any means without the written permission of the publisher.

Cataloging-in-Publication Data

Names: Dufresne, Emilie.
Title: Pop art / Emilie Dufresne.
Description: New York : Enslow Publishing, 2022. | Series: In my gallery | Includes glossary and index.
Identifiers: ISBN 9781978524156 (pbk.) | ISBN 9781978524170 (library bound) | ISBN 9781978524163 (6 pack) | ISBN 9781978524187 (ebook)
Subjects: LCSH: Pop art--Juvenile literature. | Art, Modern--20th century--Juvenile literature.
Classification: LCC N6494.P6 D843 2022 | DDC 709.04'071--dc23

Designer: Danielle Rippengill
Editor: Madeline Tyler

Printed in the United States of America

CPSIA compliance information: Batch #CS22ENS: For further information contact Enslow Publishing, New York, New York at 1-800-398-2504

IMAGE CREDITS

COVER AND THROUGHOUT – ARTBESOURO, APRIL_PIE, SHTONADO, TASHANATASHA, QUARTA, IRA CVETNAYA. BACKGROUNDS – EXPRESSVECTORS. CHLOE & ARTISTS – GRINBOX. GALLERY – GOODSTUDIO, SIBERIAN ART. 5 – GRINBOX, TARTILA, ARARAT.ART. 6&7 – QUARTA. 8 – WATERCOLOR_SWALLOW. 9 – IVAN LUKYANCHUK, ANATOLIR, GRAPHIC DESIGN, JASON WINTER. 10 – PRIMSKY. 11 – ROI AND ROI, ILKAYALPTEKIN. 14&15 – GRAPHIC DESIGN, JASON WINTER, LERA EFREMOVA. 22&23 – RVECTOR, GAL AMAR. 26&27 – WOWOMNOM. 28 – TRINET UZUN, ARTEMISIA1508, MASCHA TACE, PERUNIKA. 29 – TARTILA, GAL AMAR. IMAGES ARE COURTESY OF SHUTTERSTOCK.COM. WITH THANKS TO GETTY IMAGES, THINKSTOCK PHOTO, AND ISTOCKPHOTO.

CONTENTS

Page 4   Welcome to the Gallery
Page 5   Types of Art
Page 6   Pop Art Wing
Page 8   What Is Pop Art?
Page 12 Robert Rauschenberg
Page 14 Activity: Collect and Collage
Page 16 Andy Warhol
Page 18 Activity: Pop Art Portraits
Page 20 Roy Lichtenstein
Page 22 Activity: Comic Strips and Captions
Page 24 Yayoi Kusama
Page 26 Activity: Wild About Polka Dots
Page 28 Opening Night
Page 30 Quiz
Page 31 Glossary
Page 32 Index

Words that look like **this** are explained in the glossary on page 31.

WELCOME TO THE GALLERY

Hey there! My name is Chloe and I'm going to teach you all about galleries and art. I am a **specialist** in a type of art called Pop Art, and this is the gallery I work in. So let's get started with the basics...

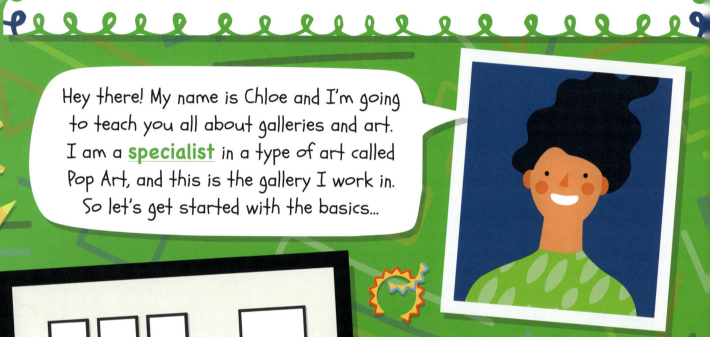

Museums and Galleries

You might have seen art in a museum or gallery. Museums and galleries buy, or are given, art to show to the public. They also look after the art so that people in years to come can still see the art and learn from it.

TYPES OF ART

There are lots of different types of art that you may find in an art gallery. Let's take a look at some of the ones we will be seeing today.

Screen printing is when paint is spread over a **stencil** and onto a **canvas**. You can layer the paint and use different stencils to create different effects. For example, Andy Warhol made screen prints of a famous woman named Marilyn Monroe.

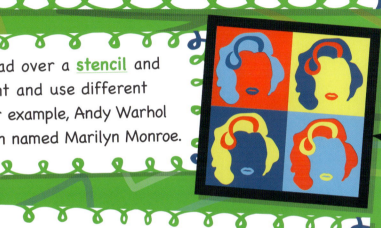

Sculpture is when a material, such as metal, stone, or wood, is molded or put together to create a 3D object. Kusama's pumpkin sculptures are an example of this.

Photography is when artists use cameras to take photographs of people or things to create art. Rauschenberg used photographs in his **assemblage** and **collage** pieces.

POP ART WING

It's looking a bit empty. But don't worry – you're here to help me make some amazing art in the Pop Art style for the exhibition's opening night.

A museum or gallery may have different floors or areas. These areas may have a certain type of art, such as art from one artist or art from one **movement**. This wing is going to be full of Pop Art.

I think we need some large prints on that wall – with some sculptures right in the middle of the room and maybe even an installation at the end. This is going to be one of the brightest and boldest wings in the gallery!

AN INSTALLATION ARTWORK COULD TAKE UP AN ENTIRE ROOM, AND THE PUBLIC HAS TO EXPERIENCE IT RATHER THAN JUST LOOK AT IT. THIS MEANS YOU MAY HAVE TO WALK AROUND IT OR TOUCH IT.

Now it's time to learn all about Pop Art. Let's get started.

WHAT IS POP ART?

Before Pop Art

Before Pop Art, there was an art movement called Abstract Expressionism. Abstract Expressionism was less about painting people or things and more about trying to show thoughts or feelings. Artists did this by using different colors and using new and interesting ways of putting paint onto the canvas.

JACKSON POLLOCK WAS AN ABSTRACT EXPRESSIONIST WHO MADE PAINTINGS BY FLICKING AND POURING PAINT ONTO A CANVAS, LIKE THIS.

Abstract Expressionist artists would often let their feelings change how the painting looked. They might drip, spray, or brush the paint onto the canvas.

Against Abstract Expressionism

Pop Art first started in Great Britain in the 1950s and in the U.S. in the 1960s. Unlike the Abstract Expressionist artists, Pop Art wasn't really about feelings. It was more about **replicating** things that the public saw all the time.

This was often things in the **media**, such as ads, celebrities, and everyday items. Pop Art artists used everyday items, such as things from grocery stores, as well as images from TV and ads, to create art that could be put into galleries and museums. This made people look at these things in a different way.

Borrow and Choose

Pop Art was known for its use of bright and bold colors. The images that were used were often shown in the same way that the media showed them in **popular culture**. This is where the "pop" in Pop Art is from.

Pop Art artists used the brightly colored pictures and bold lettering that was used in ads, comic strips, and on TV. Some artists would only focus on one image or object in their work while others would look at the media as a whole.

Making Art Popular

Pop Art became very popular in the 1960s. It was an important art movement because it was enjoyed by many people in the public and not just people who knew a lot about art. This was because it contained things that the public could understand and recognize. This wasn't always the case with art in galleries. Even today, there are many artists still creating popular art in the style of Pop Art from the 1950s and '60s. For example, Jeff Koons and Yayoi Kusama are both examples of artists who use the Pop Art style today.

JEFF KOONS HAS MADE VERY LARGE AND VERY BRIGHT SCULPTURES THAT LOOK LIKE GIGANTIC CHILDREN'S TOYS, SUCH AS MODELING CLAY AND BALLOON ANIMALS.

ROBERT RAUSCHENBERG

Country of Birth: U.S.
Born: 1925
Died: 2008 (aged 82)

Robert Rauschenberg was making art in the Pop Art style before it became a movement. From early on in his career, he started using everyday items such as newspapers, soda bottles, and stuffed animals in his artworks. He used these in assemblage pieces. During the Pop Art movement, he began to experiment with the use of newspapers, photographs, and paint in his collages. He called these "combines," as they combined many different art styles in one piece of art.

Rauschenberg kept developing his style of combines throughout the 1950s and 1960s, and even borrowed Andy Warhol's screen-printing techniques to **transfer** photos onto canvas. Often, these collages had pictures and text overlapping each other with bold paint strokes going over the top of them.

Activity:
COLLECT AND COLLAGE

You will need:

- Strong paper or cardboard ☑
- Brightly colored paints ☑
- Newspapers and magazines ☑
- Photographs ☑
- Scissors ☑
- Glue ☑
- Paintbrushes ☑

It's time to make a collage in the style of Rauschenberg. Let's get cutting and gluing!

Go through magazines and newspapers and cut or rip out any pictures, headlines, or articles.

Now arrange them on the page, but don't glue them down yet!

Arrange the pieces until you are happy with where they are. Now glue them down. Make sure you think about which pieces of paper you want at the front of your collage and glue them down last.

Wait until the glue is dry. Now it's time for the fun part – painting! Choose a bright color and use a very large paintbrush.

Brush the paint in streaks over any part of your collage that you want to. It doesn't matter if it covers the words and picture – go wild! Leave it to dry and there you have it – your very own collage!

ANDY WARHOL

Country of Birth: U.S.
Born: 1928
Died: 1987 (aged 58)

Andy Warhol may be the most famous Pop Art artist. He became famous for painting and drawing pictures of everyday household items such as soup cans, and for making sculptures by recreating the packaging of cleaning products. He also created prints of famous celebrities such as Marilyn Monroe. He would make many copies of these paintings and sculptures by using mechanical methods similar to those you might find in a factory.

In fact, Warhol's workshop became known as The Factory because he used screen-printing methods and paid art assistants to help him create his work much like a factory would. At that time, many people did not see this as a method of art, because the artist, Andy Warhol, did not always make the art himself. However, many others saw this as a revolutionary way of making art, as it copied the mass production method that was being used during the 1960s.

16

Activity:
POP ART PORTRAITS

You will need:

- Brightly colored paints ✓
- Printouts of the same photo of someone's face ✓
- A pencil ✓
- Paintbrushes ✓
- Sheets of thick paper ✓

Find a picture of someone's face you want to use. I'm using myself, but you could choose anyone.

Print this picture out at least four times on thick paper.

Take all the photos and draw around any of the features on the face and head. These could be the lips, teeth, eyes, eyebrows, or hair.

Now use different colors to paint different areas of the photograph.

Do this again and again until you have lots of different paintings of the same photo.

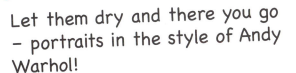

Let them dry and there you go – portraits in the style of Andy Warhol!

I can't wait to see how these look in the gallery. How did yours go?

19

ROY LICHTENSTEIN

Country of Birth: U.S.
Born: 1923
Died: 1997 (aged 73)

Roy Lichtenstein was a Pop Art artist who was famous for recreating comic strips and comic book images in his paintings. He often created the images on a much larger scale and made them have more impact by being bolder and brighter.

He used a technique in his paintings in which he would place lots of dots on the page. This was a technique he borrowed from comic book and newspaper printing. Depending on the color and spacing between the dots, different colors and shades could be made. However, in Lichtenstein's paintings, these dots became a lot bigger and a lot easier to see as dots rather than just shading. These dots became an iconic part of his work. He would also use bold onomatopoeic words such as WHAM, CRACK, and BLAM.

Activity:
COMIC STRIPS AND CAPTIONS

You will need:

- Brightly colored paint ☑
- Black paint ☑
- Thick cardboard or a canvas ☑
- Paintbrushes ☑
- A pencil ☑
- A ruler ☑

I NEVER THOUGHT I'D S

First, choose an object you want to draw, such as a person's face, an airplane, or an explosion!

Draw a quick **sketch** of how you want it to look all together.

Don't forget you can add big onomatopoeic words or longer captions. I think I might go for WOW and OMG!

Now paint in the areas with bright, bold colors — be careful not to go over the lines!

Set your painting aside to dry and start to think about the shading.

Now it's time to outline all of your painting with black lines.

You can add dots anywhere that you want to look more shaded, or add a caption like in a comic book.

23

YAYOI KUSAMA

Country of Birth: Japan
Born: 1929

In the 1960s, Yayoi Kusama worked alongside Pop Art artists of the time such as Andy Warhol and Roy Lichtenstein. She is still producing Pop Art artworks today. Kusama is an artist who has worked with many different art forms in her life, including painting, sculpture, installations, and **performance art**. Throughout her lifetime, she has been obsessed with polka dots, mirrors, and pumpkins. These objects appear in many of her pieces. She often uses **hallucinations** that she had as a child as **inspiration** for her works.

Kusama uses mirrors and lights in her work to create installations that feel as though they go on forever. In one installation, *Obliteration Room*, Kusama created a room that was completely white – even the furniture was white. On entering the room, visitors were given polka dot stickers that they could use to cover the white space. Kusama is still creating bright, dotty, pumpkin-filled art to this day.

Activity:
WILD ABOUT POLKA DOTS

You will need:

A pumpkin (any size)

Black paint

Brightly colored paint

A paintbrush

To begin, wash off any mud or dirt from your pumpkin and dry it with a clean towel.

Choose any brightly colored paint and paint your pumpkin! I have chosen to use red! You might have to do this in two stages to let the paint completely dry before painting the bottom.

Now use the black paint to make different-sized dots over your pumpkin, like this: ● ● ● ·

Now let it dry and there you go – your very own dotty pumpkin!

Bonus – Spotty Installation

Take a cardboard box and paint it white inside and out.

Now get your friends together and get them to help you cover the box in colored dot stickers.

Now you have your very own installation artwork!

It's important to talk about how art makes you feel and whether you like it or not. Why not take a look at the pieces of art you made and try answering these questions. Do you like it? Why do you, or don't you, like it?

QUIZ

1. Other than showing art to the public, what do museums and galleries aim to do?

2. What technique did Robert Rauschenberg use to make his combines?

3. Which two Pop Art artists used a technique called screen printing?

4. Which artist used comic strips as their inspiration?

5. Who created the installation artwork *Obliteration Room*?

Answers: 1. Look after the art for people to see in years to come **2.** Collage **3.** Robert Rauschenberg and Andy Warhol **4.** Roy Lichtenstein **5.** Yayoi Kusama

Why not go and visit an art gallery or museum near you?

Art galleries and museums will have lots of different artworks from different times and movements. You never know – it might inspire you to create your own things, just like we have done here. Don't forget to talk about how the art makes you feel when you are there.

GLOSSARY

assemblage — a type of art that can look like a sculpture or installation in which different objects are assembled together to make one whole piece

canvas — a woven fabric that is pulled tightly over a frame to create a blank space to be painted on

collage — a type of art where different materials and objects are glued onto a surface

hallucinations — dream-like experiences where you see, hear, or feel things that aren't in the real world

iconic — when something is well known and a symbol of a place or time

inspiration — something that gives a person ideas to create something such as art, music, or poetry

mass production — a quick and cheap way of producing large amounts of one product that all look nearly identical

media — the different ways that information is shown to the public such as TV, advertisements, newspapers, and radio

movement — a category or type of art that an artwork or artist might belong to, which can sometimes be related to a certain time or place

onomatopoeic — when a word sounds like the thing it is describing, such as "bang" or "moo"

performance art — a type of art that is often performed live for viewers or spectators

popular culture — culture such as music, art, fashion, TV, and film that is enjoyed and liked by the majority of a population

replicating — producing almost exact copies

revolutionary — doing something in a way that drastically changes how it was done or thought of before

sketch — to do a quick drawing, often in pencil

specialist — someone who is very knowledgeable in one particular area

stencil — a sheet that has a pattern or shape cut out of it that can help to create screen prints

transfer — to move from one place to another

INDEX

A
Abstract Expressionism 8–9
ads 9
assemblages 5, 12

C
canvases 5, 8, 12, 22
celebrities 9, 16
collages 5, 12, 14–15
comics 10, 20

F
factories 16

G
galleries 4–7, 9, 11, 19

I
installations 7, 24, 27, 29

M
media 9–10

P
paint 5, 8, 12, 14–16, 18–20, 22–24, 26–28
photographs 5, 12, 14, 18–19
pictures 10, 12, 15–16, 19, 28
polka dots 24, 27
pumpkins 5, 24, 26–27

S
sculpture 5–7, 11, 16, 24, 28
stickers 24, 27

T
TV 9–10